Caterpillar Jo and the Seasons

Written by Kelly Titcombe
Illustrated by Aniqa Siddiq

First edition published 2022

Great Britain

For further copies of this book please email

caterpillarjo3@gmail.com

Dedication

I would like to firstly thank Him, the one who inspired each word and picture of this book.

I would also like to thank my family and friends for their loving support and encouragement along the way.

Thank you to Laila Sennah for editing this book.

One cool day in a lovely garden, Caterpillar Jo was talking to Mama Butterfly.

"What will happen when I grow up?" asked Caterpillar Jo. "I want to go on an adventure and fly high like you!"

"Oh, you will one day but first pay attention to all the things around you and remember what you enjoy now." replied Mama Butterfly.

So off Caterpillar Jo went...

In January, Caterpillar Jo had fun building a snowman as the crispy, icy snowflakes settled.

It was really cold.

But Caterpillar Jo kept going. Next month will he keep growing?

In February, Caterpillar Jo travelled through a forest. It was rather quiet as many animals were fast asleep.

It was still quite cold.

But Caterpillar Jo kept going. Next month will he keep growing?

In March, Caterpillar Jo gazed at a beautiful, colourful rainbow. Raindrops fell and landed to make wet, splashy puddles along the path.

It was beginning to feel warmer.

But Caterpillar Jo kept going. Next month will he keep growing?

In April, Caterpillar Jo rested peacefully and asked toad "What does a water lilly taste like? Have you ever eaten a lotus leaf before?"

It was feeling much warmer.

But Caterpillar Jo kept going. Next month will he keep growing?

In May, Caterpillar Jo sat by a lake and listened to the croaking frogs "ribbet, ribbet". Sycamore seeds spiralled gently to the ground as Caterpillar Jo ate a delicious lunch.

As the sun set, Caterpillar Jo climbed up a tree to look closely at the tweeting birds. It was fun being up so high.

But Caterpillar Jo kept going. Next month will he keep growing?

In June, Caterpillar Jo went to a fruit farm. The sweet scent of the summer fruits made Caterpillar Jo hungry so some strawberries were picked to eat. Yummy!

It was feeling quite hot.

But Caterpillar Jo kept going. Next month will he keep growing?

In July, Caterpillar Jo built a sandcastle using a bucket and spade then sunbathed by the ocean. The cold ice-cream was scrumptious.

Caterpillar Jo strolled along the pier for a swim in the refreshing ocean. Seagulls squawked and Caterpillar Jo thought about flying one day.

It was now feeling scorching hot.

But Caterpillar Jo kept going. Next month will he keep growing?

In August, Caterpillar Jo wriggled up the stem of a giant sunflower. Mmmm... the smell of lavender and roses felt soothing. Caterpillar Jo was having a really good time as the skies were clear and the busy bees buzzed.

But Caterpillar Jo kept going. Next month will he keep growing?

In September, Caterpillar Jo saw Mama Butterfly.

"Have you been enjoying yourself?" she asked. "Remember to always cherish these moments, especially in difficult times."

In October, Caterpillar Jo crawled along a damp tree branch and tried to catch a crunchy, golden leaf but the strong wind blew it away and it landed in the river.

It was getting cooler.

But Caterpillar Jo kept going. Next month will he keep growing?

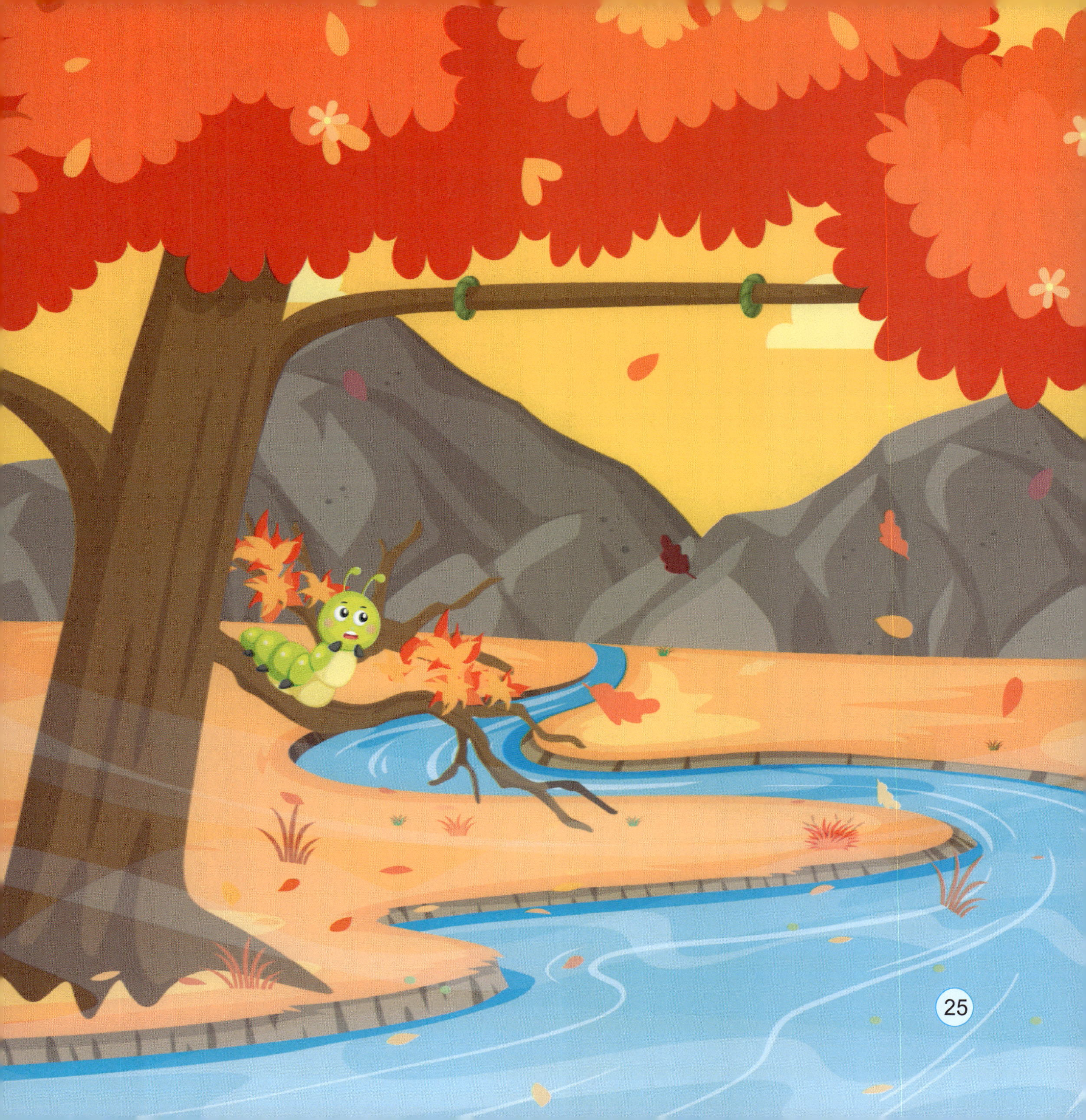

In November, Caterpillar Jo noticed a flock of birds flying away. They were migrating. Caterpillar Jo tried to follow them but got caught up in a thunder storm.

It was cold and wet.

But Caterpillar Jo kept going. Next month will he keep growing?

In December, Caterpillar Jo decorated a Christmas tree with baubles whilst drinking a delicious cup of hot chocolate. The fire crackled. Caterpillar Jo began to feel really tired and sluggish.

Feeling rather sleepy, Caterpillar Jo clambered up a branch, snuggled under a comfy leaf and fell fast asleep.

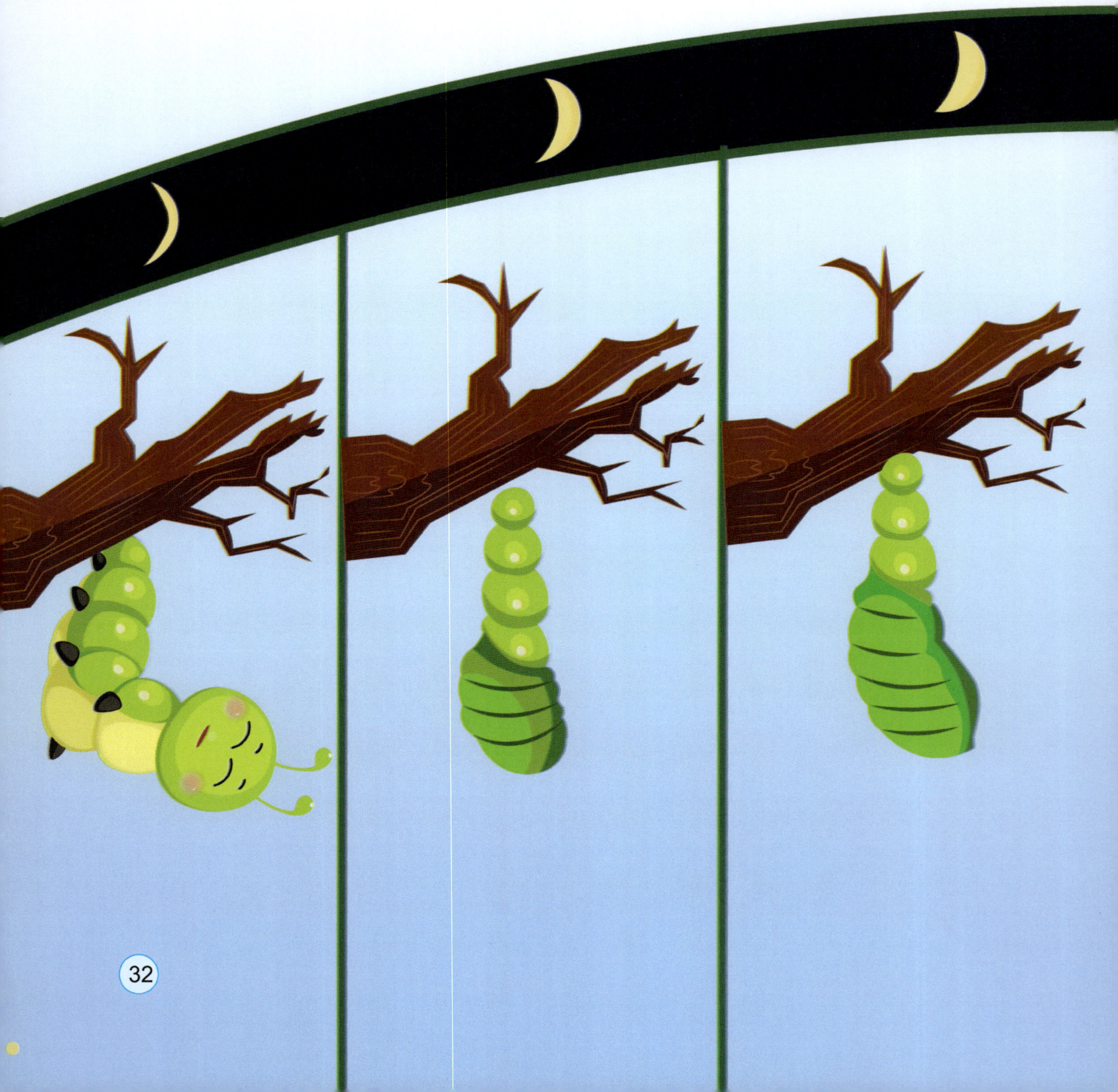

It was very dark in the chrysalis. Caterpillar Jo felt lonely in the pitch black cocoon.

"Is anybody there?"

Caterpillar Jo felt shaky and heard the echo of his voice.

Caterpillar Jo remembered what Mama Butterfly had said.

"Remember to always cherish these moments, especially in difficult times."

Suddenly, rays of bright light came bursting through the darkness. Caterpillar Jo was excited.

"What is this? I feel different. I look different. I can flap and I can fly!"

Butterfly Jo fluttered and flew high up into the sky along with the bees, wasps and other butterflies. The world looked different from this new view and Butterfly Jo was happy to be grown.

Optional comprehension questions for parents to use:

pg. 4:
-What does Caterpillar Jo want to do?
-Who is Mama Butterfly?
-Where are they?

pg. 6:
-What settled on the ground?
-What is he building?
-Have you ever seen or made a snowman?
-How is he feeling?

pg. 8:
-Where is Caterpillar Jo?
-Why were the animals asleep?
-What else can you see (in the picture)?

pg. 10:
-How did he look at the rainbow?
-What made the puddle?
-Why is there a rainbow?/How did a rainbow appear?

pg. 12:
-What is a lotus/water lily?
-What do you think water lilies and lotus leaves taste like?
-What is the weather like here in April?

pg. 14:
-What did Caterpillar Jo hear as he sat by the lake?
-Where are the sycamore seeds in the picture?
-Why/how are they falling to the ground?

pg. 15:
-Why does Caterpillar Jo think it is fun to climb a tree?
-What sounds can he hear up in the tree?

pg. 16:
-What can he smell in the fruit farm?
-How did this make him feel?
-Why do you think he is wearing a hat?

pg. 18:
-How did he build a sandcastle?
-What did he do by the ocean?
-What did the ice-cream taste like?
-Have you ever eaten ice-cream?/ what is your favourite flavour?

pg. 19:
-How did Caterpillar Jo walk along the pier?
-What made him think about flying one day?
-What is the weather like here?

pg. 20:
-What is Caterpillar Jo climbing up now?
-Why is he having a good time?
-What is making him feel relaxed?

pg. 22:
-What does Mama Butterfly ask Caterpillar Jo?
-What do you think will be his answer?
-What do you think the word 'cherish' means?

pg. 24:
-What does the tree branch feel like to Caterpillar Jo?
-What was he trying to do on the tree?
-Where did it land?

pg. 26:
-Why are the flock of birds flying away?
-Why did he not follow the birds?
-How do you think he is feeling now?

pg. 28:
-What is he decorating the christmas tree with?
-What sounds can he hear?
-How is he feeling?

pg. 30:
-How did he climb the tree?
-What did he do under the leaf?
pgs. 32-33:
Discuss the different stages of the chrysalis being formed.Refer to the different phases of the moon to discuss time passing
(crescent moon, half moon, full moon etc.)

pg. 34:
-Why is it very dark?
-What sounds can Caterpillar Jo hear?
-What is an echo?
-How is he feeling?

pg. 36:
-How did Caterpillar Jo stop feeling lonely and shaky?
-What memories did he think of?
-How do you stop yourself from ever feeling sad and lonely?

pg. 38:
-What happened to make him feel excited?
-What are the 'rays' of bright light?

pg. 40:
-What happened to him?
-How does he look different?
-What can he do now that he couldn't do before?

pg. 42:
-What is the butterfly's name?
-Why does everything look different to him now?
-What word tells us that he is flapping his wings?
-Where do you think he is going?

Guided Reading – Planning Sheet (for teachers)

Band – These questions and text is suitable for the expected reading level at Year 2 (UK)

Y/N = Yes/No FW = Find Word FP = Find Phrase I = Inference AK = Applied Knowledge

Book introduction	**Look at the front cover. Relate to children's experiences.** Have you ever seen a caterpillar? Where did you see the caterpillar? What do you know about caterpillars?
Strategy check	• NO READING FINGER. • What should you do if you come to a word that you can't read? Segment and blend together. • If you come to a large word what should you do? Find chunks of words within the word or find small words in big words. • What should you do if you come to a sentence that doesn't make sense? Read the sentence again. • What should you do if it still doesn't make sense? Read the sentence before and after. • What should you do if you see speech marks? • What should you do if you come to a comma?
Independently reading to given pages and then responding to questions.	• Check that children are using strategies – ask them to show you. • Early finishers to be seated next to each other and partner read (can use fingers now for partner to follow). • Remind the children when asking questions that they must put their fingers underneath the answer and not call out. **Read to page: 8** 1. What kind of garden was Caterpillar Jo in? lovely FW 2. Do you think Caterpillar Jo will ever fly high? Why? AK 3. Where did the snowflakes settle? I 4. Why do you think the animals were fast asleep? AK **Read to page: 14** 5. How did Caterpillar Jo look at the raindrops? gazed FW 6. Why was it beginning to feel warm in March? AK 7. Do you think toad liked the taste of water lilies or lotus leaves? I – discussion question 8. What were the frogs doing? croaking FW 9. Where did the sycamore seeds fall from? The trees AK – discussion questions **Read to page :18** 10. Where is the sun in the sky when the sun sets? AK 11. Where were the birds? I

Independently reading to given pages and then responding to questions.	12. Why was it feeling hot in June? AK 13. What word describes how the ice-cream tasted? Scrumptious FW **Read to page : 24** 1. Can you point to the pier in the picture? 2. How did Caterpillar walk to the pier? strolled FW 3. What did Mama Butterfly remind him to do? FP 4. Why was the tree branch damp? I **Read to end** 5. Where were the birds going? AK 6. How did Caterpillar Jo climb up the branch in December? clambered FW 7. Why was Caterpillar Jo feeling shaky? I 8. On Page 36 why did he remember what Mama Butterfly said to him? I 9. Who is Butterfly Jo? Child should associate with Caterpillar Jo. I

Printed in Great Britain
by Amazon

21699589R00029